Unplug Me Now

A novella

Prologue

He ran as fast as he could as they were closing in on him by foot. They have him well covered; there is certainly no escape for him now. The countless helicopters up in the sky had zeroed in on him and police vehicles had sealed the streets. Any shots fired now would kill him instantly. "I was only trying to save them," he thought to himself. The very people he was trying to free are the ones that want to kill him. He could not believe how stupid humans are. He wondered why his brother hadn't unplugged him yet. He was out of options and he knew he wasn't going to survive the jump he was about to make. Even if he survives the leap, he would not escape the gun shots. He jumped regardless, and the bullets came raining down.

It all began in Unus, a universe that has reached the apex of any possible advancement. In that universe, everyone can create anything they want and their aircraft can travel faster than the speed of light. Life is quite boring however because there is no incentive for anyone to play professional sports or partake in any form of activities just to entertain others. For fun, they create simulated universe and watch it with excitement. Everyone in that universe has his own simulated universe.

The simulator of our universe...well, we don't know his name, so we will call him NP had grown from his love of simulating dinosaurs to his love for simulating humans. NP and his brother (we will call his brother JP) were the first in Unus to create a medium whereby they can become characters in their own simulation. They both wanted to take their excitement to the next level, and they convinced each other to become characters in their simulation. The plan had only one drawback: DEATH. If you die in the simulation, you also die in Unus unless you were unplugged. JP would go first and NP will go later. The goal was to observe their stimulation from within after which they have to convince the characters in the simulation that they are in a simulation. "I doubt if they will believe," NP had thought. He had given the characters somewhat of a control and he knew that they will never buy it that they are not in control of their lives. The illusion of control had made the simulation so much more fun for nobody likes that fact that they are not in control of their destiny.

JP was to enter our universe as a nobody for that will make the job a lot harder and much more fun. NP didn't want to make him the president of US, Russia or China for that will make the job a lot easier even though he is so convinced that they still won't buy it that they are living in a cosmic mathematical stimulation. "Even if I make him president of all three countries, they still won't believe," he thought to himself. The illusion of control was a key part of every simulation; without it, the simulation will fail. JP was also to wait till he turned 18 earth years before he can begin his mission.

JP was born on February 2nd 2002 in San Francisco to a middle class family. His dad was a high school football coach and his mom was a high school teacher. They both work at Abraham Lincoln high school in San Francisco, California. His parents had tried for years to have a child and when they finally gave birth to him, they named him Fortune, for they said he will bring fortune to the world.

At the age of 18, Fortune was already sick and tired of this world. He couldn't wait to get out. The simulated universe was not as fun as he had anticipated. From the outside, he had enjoyed watching people destroy their lives and watching people panic when a force destroys their properties but from the inside, it was a different ballgame. Seeing the pain of people suffering touched him even though he knows it's not real. He made up his mind to shut down his simulation once he gets unplugged. "I will find something else to do for fun," he imagined. He was amazed by how much effort people put in other to be successful on earth without them even knowing that they have already be programmed. Their success or failure doesn't really depend on them. They have already been programmed even before they were born. They have no control whatsoever on most occurrence in the Universe. He was determined more than ever to succeed in the mission and quickly leave this world.

He had called the CIA and arranged a meeting with them. At first, they didn't take him seriously until he told them a lot of their secrets. "How did he know all this?" they wondered. They agreed to meet with him and he requested that he wants to speak to the President. The president of the United States at that time was a man named Donald Trump. His winning the presidency had shocked the world. Trump didn't have time for Fortune's bullshit, till the CIA told him all the information that Fortune had. "How did he get all that information?" Trump asked. "We don't know," the agents replied. He said all he wants is to speak with you privately. "Okay, I will meet with him, and we will kill him afterwards because if his information goes out, the CIA and America is doomed," Trump replied. He then proceeded to say that this is a matter of national security.

Fortune had underestimated the narrow mindedness of man. His plan was to convince Trump and make Trump persuade Putin and together they can convince the world that they were living in a cosmic mathematical simulation and his mission is done. He couldn't be so wrong.

The CIA had mapped out a detailed plan on how they would take out Fortune as soon as his meeting with Trump was over. They couldn't risk having someone like him in the world.

Fortune met with Trump in the white house on February 5th 2020; he couldn't believe how orange Trump was. He had remembered when his brother was creating the Trump character. "I would make this strange looking guy the president of the United States some day and it will send shock-waves across Earth," His brother had said. His brother had made Trump a bold, self-centred business man but his ultimate success was to come from his ability to notice minute things that 99.9% of humans will miss. He was to make Trump come across like a 4th grader but tacitly smart, racist and brave. Over the years, Trump also became really good in creating media attention for himself. Americans loved boldness and are so concerned about the day to day lives of their celebrities. Nothing is more thrilling to an American than seeing a celebrity go down. Those words, YOU ARE FIRED on the celebrity apprentice show was to lead trump to success and he knew it.

Trump knew Barrack Obama was born in the United States but he insinuated that Barrack wasn't born in America and he went at him hard. He doubled down on that suggestion everyday even when members of the Republican party asked him to back down. He did that so that he could obtain the trust of the conservative base because their most hated celebrity was Obama. With that, Trump quickly became their GOD and there was no stepping down now. He had also demanded to see Obama's academic records because he thought Obama would have claimed citizenship of a foreign nation in other to get financial benefits from the University. Trump tried everything he could behind closed doors to obtain those records.

Trump was going to run against Obama in 2012 but he quickly backed down after Obama sabotaged him at the 2011 white house correspondents dinner. Trump had been given a special invitation and he thought he would be given a VIP treatment at the dinner. He has an innate ability to sense fear and he was astonished by how bold Obama was. Instantly, he knew Obama would destroy him on the debate stage. Nothing would have been more devastating to Trump than for a black man to defeat him.

Trump lived by some certain principles which works for him. Some of those principles include: Never apologize even if you are wrong, never accept responsibility for failure even if it is your fault, even in failure, just say you succeeded. You can achieve that by courageously twisting the facts or finding a little thing you succeeded in that failure and brag about it. It's wise to note that our brains secretly likes Trump whether we know it or not.

While running against Hilary Clinton in 2016, Trump heard words that the Russians were trying to help him win the elections and he loved it. He wilily asked the Russians during one of his campaign speeches to obtain the deleted emails from Hilary Clinton's Server. He knew they will obtain it in time right before election week.

Up to election day, Trump was behind in the polls but he kept saying he was ahead. He had his code but even him could not believe it when he finally won on election night. He knew he had a chance but this came as a surprised to him. He hadn't written any victory speech and he had plans on how he would challenge the election results and question the legitimacy of Hilary Clinton's Presidency. "Only if he knew the simulator's game", Fortune had thought in his living room. In the next couple of months, the simulator was to make a guy that looks exactly like Trump, the prime minister of Britain. Weird world, indeed!

The simulator needed Trump to be President because Trump was to anger everyone and a country will level up with him and the world with a deadly virus. Any proactive president would have prevented the United States from been infected with the virus but Trump was created to be reactive. Trump will stick to his principles by downplaying the threat of the virus until it will be too late. You can twist the facts on everything but not with an infectious disease because people will die. Fortune could remember in early 2020 as Trump kept bragging about the economy and the low unemployment numbers. "If only this guy knows what was about to hit him, he would shut up," Fortune murmured.

At the meeting with Trump, Fortune explained everything; he told Trump how the world is not really real and he wants Trump to talk to his friend, Vladimir Putin so that it can be easier to convince the world that they are in a simulation. Trump found his story enthralling but he wanted to know only one thing. "Am I going to be re-elected?" he asked. "I can't tell you that," Fortune replied. "Why?" Trump demanded. "Because my mission is to tell you that you are in a simulation and not to predict the future," he replied. "Then we are done here; I can't help you," Trump said. The simulator had made Trump a very clever negotiator but Fortune couldn't see anything beyond his 18th birthday so he couldn't be of help anyways. That was the agreement he had with his brother to make his experience on earth more fun. "This is not about helping me," he answered Trump. It's you and the world that needs help but before he could finish speaking, Trump stood up and left the room. "We are done here," Trump said on his way out. Fortune knew Trump was created to be egocentric but he could not believe the degree of self-centeredness Trump possessed. "This world is doomed," Fortune said as he made his way out of the white house.

Fortune took a taxi straight to Ronald Reagan Washington airport immediately he left the white house. The CIA followed closely ready to strike him at any moment. They researched all the things he loved and they knew he will order coffee while waiting for his flight at the airport. They had staffs all over the airport; they were going to poison his coffee. His flight was at 4pm and Fortune arrived at 2pm. "Enough time to take him out," one of the agents whispered.

As soon as Fortune got to the airport, he quickly entered into one of the bathroom. The airport was filled with people and the CIA agents were waiting for Fortune to come out of the bathroom. It's 4mins already and he still wasn't out; they know the average male stay up to 4mins in the bathroom and CIA agent Smith decided to check inside the bathroom. To his surprise, Fortune was no where to be found.

Fortune had planned his escape for years. He knew what humans are capable of. Within 40secs of entering the bathroom, he changed his clothes, came out in disguised as a different person and hurried out of the airport. He took a taxi to the Dupont Circle bus terminal in DC. Earlier that day, when his flight arrived from San Francisco to DC airport, he had gone into that same bathroom to hide some clothes and his disguise materials in the trash can. He also knows that the cleaners throw away the bathroom trash at 3pm everyday. Two weeks earlier, even before contacting the CIA, he had flown into the same airport in DC and jokingly ask the cleaner how often they clean up the bathroom. The cleaner told him everything he needed to know.

At the bus terminal, he took another taxi to the Union Station bus terminal in DC. He was going to make it harder for the CIA to track him down; he had also prepared 7 different fake IDs. He boarded a mega bus to Pittsburgh, Pennsylvania. At Cumberland, Maryland, barely 2hrs into the bus ride, police busted the mega bus Fortune had entered looking for him. Again, he was nowhere to be found. Fortune knew it would take 2hrs for the authorities to track him down and he got off 1hr earlier at the bus terminal in Frederick, Maryland. He checked into room 202 at the Hampton Inn and Suites Hotel as Rudy Maze.

Fortune laid down on his hotel bed exhausted but before he could close his eyes, the door clicked open. It was CIA agent Nick Brown, an African American man from Oxford, Mississippi. Nick had grown up poor but he was a hard worker. Racism was something Nick had never understood; he loved everyone and always wondered why people hate him just for the colour of his skin. After graduating with a degree in Physics from Olemiss, he enlisted for the army because he loves America and wanted to serve his country so bad. The gross racism in the US Military shocked Nick. "What did we do?" he had always wondered. The CIA recruited Nick after 4 years in the Military because of his hard work and intelligence.

Nick had heard of Fortune's story and he believed him. The cosmic mathematical simulation story was something that puzzled him for years. "At first, the idea that our universe is a simulation sounds like an absolute nonsense but the more you look into it, the more it sounds plausible and begins to make sense" Nick had thought to himself. He had been ordered to shoot Fortune right on sight but he had a question troubling him and he knew Fortune was the only guy that can answer that question. He would still kill him, but after he gets his answers.

Fortune was terrified as hell and he could barely move a muscle. Nick looked straight into his eyes and asked, "Tell me, why do white people hate black people so much especially in America? We are not responsible for any of the problems in this world. None! And what colour is our creator?" Fortune was taken aback by the question and he managed to smile. "The creator has no colour and white people were designed to hate black people, to hate everyone; it adds to the fun and there is nothing anyone can do about that. It does not matter if you are good or bad, rich or poor, educated or uneducated; they were designed to hate" he answered. That wasn't the answer Nick was expecting but he understood. Seven years in the CIA didn't prepare him for this moment; pointing to the windows, he told Fortune to run. As soon as Fortune was out of sight, he took his gun and shot himself.

At the CIA headquarters in Langley, Virginia, the other agents heard the news of Nick Brown's death and instantly, they understood what they were dealing with.

Fortune quickly hurried into a taxi. Just as he was about to tell the taxi driver his destination, the taxi driver pulled out a gun and two other people with guns quickly entered the car. Fortune could not believe his eyes and before he could grasp what was going on, one of the guys said, "I am agent Jones and we are members of the Canadian

Security Intelligent Services (CSIS) and Justin Trudeau would like to meet with you."

Agent Jones is the Canadian agent in charge of UFOs, aliens or any form of

extraterrestrials. He has done an extensive research on the origin of life and where humans

are heading but nothing seems to make sense. He heard about Fortune and he persuaded

Justin Trudeau to allow the CSIS protect Fortune hoping that Fortune will provide some

necessary insights to his findings.

They drove Fortune all the way to Canada and stayed at the Marriott hotel in Niagara

Falls, Canada for the night. After Fortune got a well needed sleep, they offered him

breakfast in the morning. Fortune was impressed by how polite the Canadians are. His

brother had made them this way; his brother created Canada to be a melting pot were

everyone can coexist amicably. Of course, they will have their problems, but nothing

compared to the problems in the United States and the World. Although mostly cold,

Canada was to enjoy a vast area of land. They will be blessed with sufficient mineral

resources and programmed to ensure that they never lose a war.

Over at the white house, Donald Trump heard the Canadians were helping Fortune. He

was furious as hell. "I will certainly make them pay", he exclaimed.

Fortune had been schedule to fly to Ottawa later in the afternoon to meet with Justin

Trudeau. Prime Minister Justin Trudeau wasn't really interested in the simulation theory;

like most world leaders, Trump had angered him greatly. His secret agents had been

monitoring Fortune ever since he met with Donald Trump and they have been dying to find out what he knows. Justin Trudeau was highly regarded as the exact opposite of Trump; he is proactive, calculated, thoughtful, tactical, charismatic and well loved by his people. He is actually well loved all around the world and secretly referred to as anti-Trump.

Fortune couldn't wait to meet with Justin Trudeau and Agent Jones had prepared a long list of questions about Fortune's unreal theory that Fortune needs to answer before heading for the airport. Agent Jones sat down, pulled out a piece of paper from his pocket and looked Fortune straight in the eyes, as though to say: I hope you have answers.

Before Agent Jones could ask any questions, Fortune looked at him and said, "The problem is people think is all about them. First, they thought the earth was the centre of the universe before Nicolaus Copernicus propose a theory that the earth is not; he stated that the earth revolves around the Sun. Two decades after Copernicus's death, a man by the name of Giordano Bruno not only agreed that the earth revolves around the sun but space might be infinite. He was burnt on the stake for his views. Afterwards, Galileo came along, though he knew, he mainly stayed quiet because he did not want to suffer the same fate as Giordana Bruno. It wasn't until 100 years later that scientist began to embrace Copernicus's idea. After several years, man then discovered that their solar systems is not actually "it", that there are other systems in the milky way galaxy. Shortly after that, they found out that they are also other galaxies; and here I am, telling you that other universe exist."

Agent Jones:

We cannot think in a way that we were not designed to think. We cannot see the true nature of the universe because we don't have the capacity to do so. But a huge part of us cannot help it. We need to know why we are here. Where we came from and where we are heading?

Fortune:

You came from nothing and you will return to nothing.

That answer wasn't what Agent Jones was expecting to hear. he looked at Fortune for a while and moved on to the next question.

Agent Jones:

You are saying we came from nothing and we will return to nothing. What about life after death?

Fortune

Life about what? You are not even in control of your lives here in this universe.

Agent Jones:

Are you saying that we are not in control of anything? That everything is programmed? Regardless of what we do?

Fortune:

Yes everything is fixed. Fixed fixed fixed. You are given somewhat of a control, the illusion of control as we call it but the day you are born and the day you will die is fixed. Whether you will be successful or not on earth is also fixed.

Agent Jones began to think about all the natural disasters: Earthquakes, Tornadoes, Hurricanes, Wild fires, and Sinkholes. he also thought about man-made wars and recessions because of corporate greed. Just when you think you have finally figured everything out and got your life on track, something unexpectedly happens to take everything away from you.

Agent Jones:

Saying there is nothing anybody can do is a hard pill to swallow.

Fortune:

That's the whole point of everything.

Agent Jones:

Why were Humans created to be greedy?

Fortune:

To ensure the continuity of life.

Agent Jones:

...But greed has led to so many unnecessary wars, famine and hunger.

Fortune:

...Yeah, that's part of the fun.

Agent Jones:

What about our laws of Physics? Are you trying to tell me that the laws of Physics are wrong?

Fortune:

Physics is wrong. Has always been wrong but they try to right their wrongs every single time.

Agent Jones had often wondered how perfect nature is and how fine-tuned for life earth is.

He had often said that some things are not made to be understood but it bothered him that

our bodies are composed of more bacteria than human.

Agent Jones:

Why did you come down here to help us?

Fortune:

I didn't initially come down here to help you. I came as a game; to experience first hand

what we make. To get more Fun; to want more of everything just like humans.

Agent Jones:

More of everything?

Fortune:

Yes, humans have been programmed to want more of everything they like.

Agent Jones:

How can we prove that we have been programmed?

Fortune:

Humans will never be able to prove that they have been programmed. That's why I am

here, to try to convince you.

Agent Jones

...In other words, you are telling me, that we are living in a cosmic mathematical

simulation with the illusion of control but because of our human limitations, we will not be

able to prove it? And you want us to believe you?

Fortune:

Yes I am. Humans will try, but will never be able to prove it; the Universe was designed that way. This world was built so that consciousness can be aware of itself. The last civilization was the best of all though; they got so advanced to the extent that they got it. They begged the creator not to wipe out their civilization but he did. He didn't want to take any chances.

With that answer Agent Jones finally got it. "That would explain the pyramids in Egypt," he said.

Fortune looked at him and smiled. Agent Jones had always wondered how and why the pyramids in Egypt were built. The stones used to build the pyramids were massive and some of the stones were transported from far far away. "We don't have the technology and machinery yet to build that again," he finally said.

The door suddenly opened and another agent came rushing in. "Change of plans, you will be flying to Russia to meet Vladimir Putin. The Russian president will like to meet you," he said.

Fortune couldn't believe what he was hearing. He had been trying to figure out a way to meet with Putin. "We need to leave right now," the agent demanded.

They drove Fortune to the airport at Niagara Falls. They had secured a private flight for him all the way to Moscow, Russia. Before Fortune came off the car, Agent Jones told him to be very careful because Putin is the most powerful man in the world and gave Fortune a cell phone, insisting that he calls him if he needs any help. Fortune took the cell phone and with a little grin on his face, he said, "The most powerful man right now is Xi Jinping."

Vladimir Putin had called Justin Trudeau as soon as the KGB told him about Fortune and his whereabouts. He had convinced Trudeau that Fortune wanted to meet with him and Trudeau had no choice but to let go. He would try to get his dirt's on Trump later. Putin also assured him that Fortune will be safe in Russia and that sounded quite ironic because Russia was not known for its safety.

Agent Jones couldn't stop thinking about all the creation theories he had heard in his lifetime. First, there was the big bang theory. This theory states that there was a big bang, an explosion and all of a sudden, the world was formed. He couldn't help but wonder who the scientists think they are deceiving. He knows that even the scientists know this theory cannot be true but they have to come up with something, they have to come up with an explanation of how this world was created. He kept thinking about why the scientists can't just say they don't know yet. The big bang to him really sounded ridiculous; he had often wondered what exploded, who created the materials that exploded and where did all the anti matter go since there have to be an equal amount of matter and anti-matter created.

The next theory he heard of was the inflation theory. This theory is just a little deeper than the big bang theory. You can also say this is the origin of the big bang theory. The inflation theory states that the world started small then it kept expanding and expanding and suddenly there was an explosion, a big bang. Like the big bang theory, it still couldn't explain the singularity. Agent Jones couldn't stop wondering what started small and who created that materials that started small.

Next came the string theory. To him, this was the stupidest theory of all, even though the research is still on going. The theory states that we are living in a ten dimensional world or time and nine dimensions. Out of the nine dimensions, six dimensions are cramped into one. "What in the world? How do they come up with stuffs like this? Don't this people even have anything better to do? They should tell this theory to their grandpas," he said.

Agent Jones thought he had heard it all, then came the multiverse theory. This theory is quite straight and simple. It states that anything that can happen will happen which means there is a universe where he is the richest man in the world like Bill Gates. "Why am I not in that Universe? Why am I in this stupid Universe?" he wondered.

After hearing all this theories, the only one that seems to make sense to agent Jones is the cosmic mathematical stimulation theory. Agent Jones had known for years that man does not have the intelligence and capability of proving where we came from and where we are going. He loved how Fortune was straight forward and honest with him. We are simply living in a cosmic mathematical simulation with the illusion of control but because of our human limitations, we will never be able to prove it. This makes perfect sense to agent Jones because he had often wondered why people born in a certain month often behave the same way. He concluded that it's because they have already be programmed to behave that way. He looked up and asked the creator to unplug him now for there is no point in life; no point in anything.

Fortune met with Putin at the Grand Kremlin Palace in Moscow, Russia. The western media often like to depict Putin as this demonic powerful figure but Putin looked quite normal and eager to learn like everyone else. Putin was actually fascinated to hear about his cosmic mathematical simulation story and wondered why Donald Trump wasn't interested in it. Well, unlike Trump, Putin had nothing to lose; he had rectified the Russian constitution so he could rule past 2024. Trump doesn't have such liberty. He has to run against the democratic nominee.

The democratic nominee will be Joe Biden although he doesn't know it yet. He just lost the Iowa caucus and he is not polling well in New Hampshire and Nevada but he will become the nominee because of the black vote. African Americans love Joe Biden more than any other candidate in the field and they will propel him to victory. The magic worlds for Biden will be I am an OBAMA BIDEN DEMOCRAT; the sooner he discovers the magic words, the better his campaign will be.

Trump had tried to get illegal dirt on Joe Biden. He called the president of Ukraine the same day he was exonerated by the FBI on the Russian meddling of the US elections. He felt he was untouchable now since the FBI couldn't indict him, and he decided to withhold the Ukrainian aid until they make an announcement that they are investigating Joe Biden and his son. That was seen as an abuse of power by the US congress and Trump was impeached for it. He survived the impeachment though because apart from the religious senator of Utah, Mitt Romney, the Republicans love their man.

Putin loved Fortune's story and he promised to help him convince Trump. Everyone on earth knows Trump is in Putin's pocket but Putin had one last question for Fortune. "How many other universe are there?" he asked. "Right now, they are 7.8billion universe but the number keep expanding everyday," Fortune replied and he brought out a picture of our universe and a picture of the human brain and showed it to Putin. Immediately, Putin understood. "I will get in touch with Trump as soon as possible and I will contact you first thing tomorrow," he said and majestically left the room.

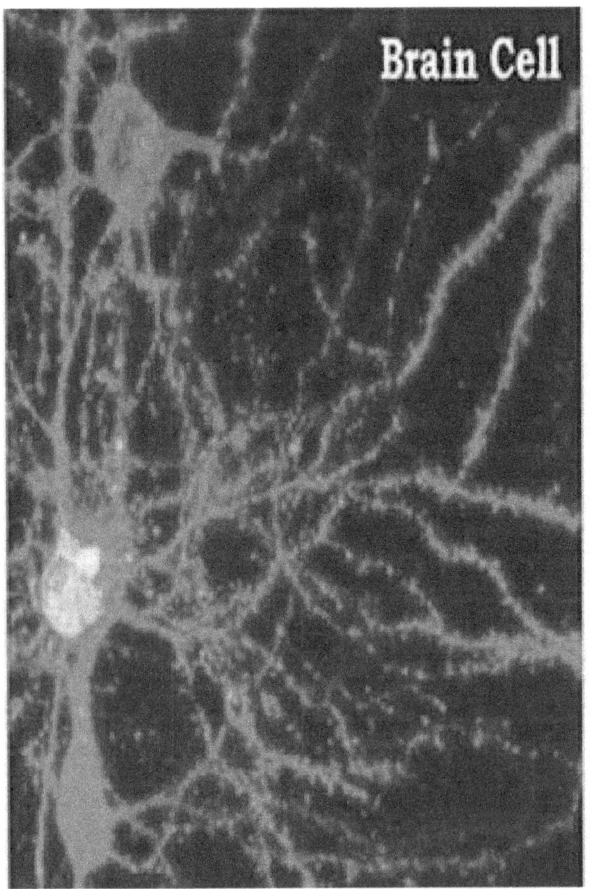

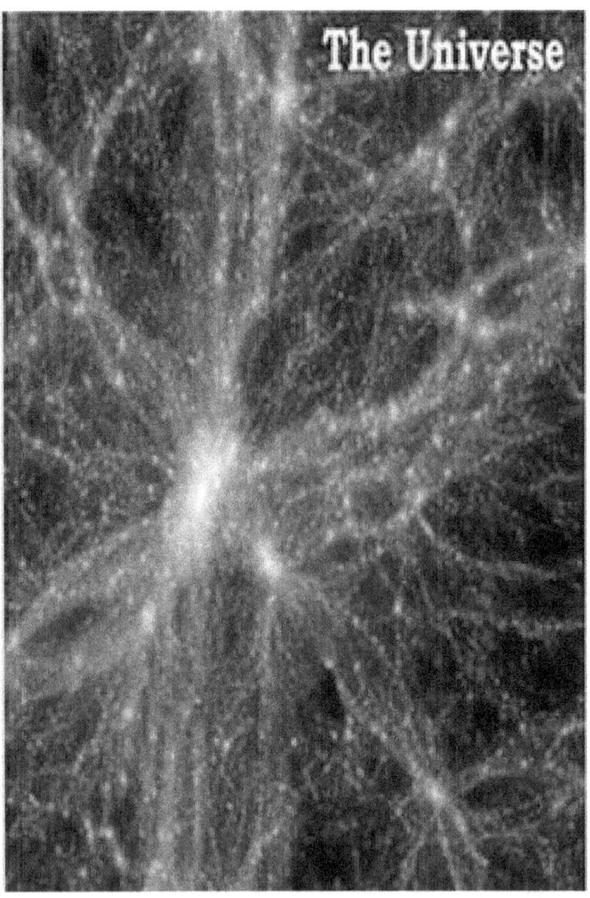

Fortune stayed at the Ritz Carlton Hotel in Moscow. That was the same hotel Trump had paid prostitutes to pee on the bed because he heard Michelle Obama and Barack Obama had stayed there earlier. Trump is such a repulsive figure and he wondered what his brother had created. Over at Unus, he would have been watching Trump with excitement, but from the inside, it actually feels disgusting.

Fortune knew Putin will succeed in talking to Trump because the only two people Trump fears in this world are Vladimir Putin and Nancy Pelosi. Nancy Pelosi is the congress woman from Fortune's district in San Francisco, California. She is currently the speaker of the house of representative in the United States. Trump usually doesn't respect women and he calls them names like Pocahontas and crooked Hilary, but with Nancy Pelosi, he doesn't have the balls to call her names; he is so scared of her. If you really want to frighten Trump, just send him a mask of Nancy Pelosi for Halloween.

The only reason Trump isn't interested in the simulation theory yet is because he is so concerned with his re-election. Trump will do anything just to get re-elected. Earlier in the year, Trump had taken out the Iranian general, Qasem Soleimani and was ready to go war with Iran just to score political points and win the upcoming elections. He was ready to risk the lives of thousands just to win an election. He knew fully well that the United States will easily defeat Iran in a war. Qasem Soleimani was no terrorist and you just don't go to kill a country's appointed official. Qasem Soleimani was the commander of the quds force and his army was widely responsible for keeping peace in the middle east. The United States army likes to take credit for defeating Isis but it's actually Qasem Soleimani's quds force that helped defeat Isis in the middle east. The world thought the Iranians will go to war with the Americans but they chickened out, knowing fully well that their military was no match for the US military.

As soon as Fortune finished his breakfast, some security officers came into the room to tell him that he will be returning to America today and Putin has talked to Trump. He was very delighted to hear the news and his mission on earth is almost complete. Fortune cannot wait to get back to Unus. Putin had arranged a first-class ticket with Aeroflot for Fortune to return to the United States.

Fortune's Aeroflot flight lasted for 11hrs. As soon as the flight landed at Ronald Reagan Washington airport in DC, police rushed into the airplane to arrest Fortune. They arrested his Russian lookalike instead, for Fortune was not in the flight. Fortune had asked Putin to let him fly earlier to New York and put someone else that looks like him on the flight to DC. Putin didn't like the idea but Fortune convinced him that he doesn't trust the US Government. He wanted to see what would happen to that person before he could proceed to meet with Trump. Putin got Fortune's Russian lookalike and the lookalike was to fly with Fortune's ID to DC.

From his Sheraton Hotel room at Niagara Falls, USA, Fortune was disgusted when he heard the news of his Russian lookalike's arrest. He had stayed at this hotel in Niagara Falls so that he could be easy for him to get into Canada just in case he needed to escape.

Right now though, he was so done with humans on earth and he looked up to the sky and asked his brother to unplug him now. His hotel room door suddenly burst open and seven Asian looking guys came gushing in. He was frighted as hell and his hands were visibly shaking. He was still waiting for his brother to unplug him before one of the Asian guys finally said they were not here to kill him. They were North Korean's spy and they wanted to know about the Wuhan Coronavirus. Fortune quickly gain his composure and smiled. He was so impressed with the North Koreans. He had mentioned the virus to Trump and Trump didn't even faze; he mentioned the virus to Putin and Putin didn't ask any follow up question about it; even Canadian agent Jones didn't ask any questions about the virus but here are people from North Korean asking about the virus. Trump even said in one of his campaign speeches that the virus will just miraculously disappear.

The virus, the next phase of the simulation, an invisible human enemy will wreck havoc on earth for more than a year. "What a fun and perfect simulation his brother had created," he sighed.

Today is February 7th 2020 and North Korea doesn't have any case of the virus. They will never have any case of the virus but the World will not believe them because they are so secretive and they don't share information. In this case though, they will be saying the truth.

Fortune sat down on the bed, looked up to the ceiling and began his narrative:
As long as you don't allow anyone into your country, you will have nothing to worry about; lock down your country right now and don't allow anybody in or out for the next 15 months. All the medical experts in the world will get it wrong and the virus will spread

like wildfire. The virus will turn most major cities into ghost-towns. Even in our globalized world, it will be puzzling that few lessons will be learned now, the early weeks of the outbreak, when the chances of containing and stopping the virus is highest. Like a line of dominoes, country after country will will be shut down. There will be a clear pattern of response from foolish leaders in many parts of the world...denial, fumbling and eventually lock-down. Man will finally begin to admit that there are some things that are beyond their control. In fact the most important things in this Universe are actually beyond their control.

They will wait until it's too late and the focus will be on flattening the curve, or slowing the virus' spread, to keep the death tolls from climbing further. You can't really blame the medical expert though because they have not experienced a virus like this before and they will use the experience from other similar pandemic to predict how it will spread.

The virus will be very contagious with an Rnought of 4-6. Meaning one person with the virus can spread it to 4-6 people. 50% of the people with the virus will be asymptomatic though, but they will be able to spread the virus too.

The virus will mainly be airborne; make sure everyone wears a mask because you will not know who has the virus or not. This is where the western world will make their greatest error; they will encourage everyone not to wear a medical mask because they are scared that the medical staffs will not have enough for themselves but they will lie to the public about it. They will tell the public that as long as they are not sick, they don't have to wear a medical mask. The virus can also spread through bodily fluids too; avoid handshakes, wash your hands frequently and avoid touching your face.

The virus will be able to last on surfaces for up to 17days and in the air for up to 3hrs. It will be so contagious that an affected person don't have to cough or sneeze before spreading it to others close by; an affected person can spread it by just breathing; make sure you practice social distancing. Everyone should stand 4meters away from each other, although the virus can travel up to 8meters if an affected person coughs or sneezes. Avoid the airport and airplanes; that will be the main breeding ground for the virus. It will also take from 2-17days for people that will develop symptoms to actually show it.

Fortune then got up, looked them straight in the eyes and said that the main job of the virus is to DESTROY ECONOMIES. A globalized recession will hit in the next couple of months. It will be a recession far greater than anything man has ever seen. Most nations especially the western nations will not survive. Do not listen to the World Health Organization because they are currently controlled by Xi Jinping and they will waste too much time calling this crisis a pandemic.

The World Health Organization (WHO) is a member of the United Nations development group. It was formed in 1948 and it's headquarters is in Geneva, Switzerland. WHO provides technical assistance to countries, sets international health standards and guidelines, and collects data on global health issues through the world health survey. The WHO has played a leading role in several role in several public health achievements, most notably the eradication of smallpox and the development of an ebola vaccine. The WHO consist of 194 member states and all of the member states except for Liechtenstein, plus the cooks island and Niue. A state becomes a full member of WHO by ratifying a treaty known as the constitution of the World Health Organization. The current director-general is Tedros Adhanom, the former minister of health of Ethiopia but somehow, Xi Jinping have him in his pocket.

The North Koreans will take to his advice but they had one more question for him. "Who created the virus and why?" they asked. Fortune was stunned by the question. Somehow the North Koreans knew that this virus was no accident or mistake. He quickly recalled when his brother was creating the North Koreans. "They have to be a place where no one knows what goes on inside," his brother had said. Although the United States have developed spy drones flying around North Korea like birds, they still won't get the picture. He finally replied them and said that any country that impose restrictions on the origin of the coronavirus...Before Fortune could finish his sentence, it hit him. "Is any one wearing a wire? Is anyone wearing a listening device?" he asked. The North Koreans looked at themselves and two of the guys raised up their hands. "Then it is too late," Fortune said as he jumped down the windows.

As soon as he jumped down, countless police officers rushed into the hotel room and from afar, they saw him running away. Fortune can see the numerous police cars in the street and he can hear the helicopters hovering towards him from the sky. Police officers on the ground also started running towards him.

As Fortune was running, he couldn't help but stop thinking if Trump had the balls to fight the country that made the coronavirus. "Let's see how bold or cowardice Trump really is. Can Trump be brave enough to go war with the country that developed the virus? Does the bully only chooses his prey when he knows that they are easy?" Fortune wondered.

The police officers were already catching up with him and Fortune was running out of breath. He knows fully well that if he dies here on earth, he will also die in Unus. "Why did I come down here," he wondered. He ran as fast as he could as they were closing in on him by foot. They have him well covered; there is certainly no escape for him now. The countless helicopters up in the sky had zeroed in on him and police vehicles had sealed the streets. Any shots fired now would kill him instantly. "I was only trying to save them," he thought to himself. The very people he was trying to free are the ones that want to kill him. He could not believe how stupid humans are. He wondered why his brother hadn't unplugged him yet. He was out of options and he knew he wasn't going to survive the jump he was about to make. Even if he survives the leap, he would not escape the gun shots. He jumped regardless, and the bullets came raining down.

THE END

Unplug Me Now. Part 2 coming out soon